A GIRL WHO HAD BEST NIGHTMARES

A COMPILATION OF REAL NIGHTMARES

ANVESHA BALIYAN

You pick up a book, flip to the dedication, and find that, once again, the author has dedicated a book to someone else, and not you.

But not this time.

Because we haven't yet met/have only a glancing acquaintance/are just crazy about each other/haven't seen each other in much too long/are in some way related/ will never meet, but will, I trust, despite that, always think fondly of each other...

This one's for you.

This one is for the beautiful soul reading it right now!

Contents

Foreword

This book is a compilation of real nightmares that the author of the book had. Interestingly, these dreams conveyed to her some messages that helped her in real life. This book is a result of that. She is a mysterious person and it's always a surprise when we get to know more about her.

This book has stories of different flavors but the readers will find a hint of thrill and horror in every narrative. This characteristic of the book makes it stand out from the crowd.

Preface

I usually do have tons of nightmares, just as everybody does. I know nothing is new about that. But have you ever experienced any of your dream or nightmare come true? Mysteriously, I have many!

Many of these are related to my past, some to my present, and some even showed my future! Dreams, not daydreams, are said to have connections with the higher world, our past life, or maybe also divine. Well, who knows?

In our everyday life, we run in a race of chasing this and that, then at the end of the day, comes the most necessary and desired part, which is a safe and sound slumber. I am no different. I love having a deep and undisturbed sleep for at least eight hours. I love to see dreams of my choice and get rejuvenated when I wake up. I have learned to customize my dreams, and you can also do that. It's not brainy.

Just relax and lay down straight. Enjoy the softness and comfort of your bed, mattress, pillows, quilt, and the breeze provided by your fan or AC. Then take a deep breath and relax. Repeat. Now give the command to your mind about the kind of dream you want to have. It is just like you giving the order for your pizza.

If you ask me about my favorite dream, my answer would be of any serene landscape or any celebrity having a cup of coffee with me.

But recently I have got a new way. I command myself to give book writing Ideas and related things. Isn't it amazing?

Acknowledgements

Primarily, I want to express my gratitude to my readers for purchasing and reading this book. I am grateful to you, yes the one who is reading this right now.

Thanks to my parents, undoubtedly for making me who I am. I am grateful to all my mentors and teachers for making me capable and perspicacious. I am thankful to my younger brother, who is always my inspiration to do something new and odd. I am grateful to the almighty for the blessings.
Thank you, Universe.

Prologue

This entire book is a compilation of nightmares and horrible dreams that a girl named Avni used to have. Since we naturally wake up in between a night of terror, a few stories might sound incomplete, but that's the beauty of these stories.

CHAPTER ONE

A Queer Agreement

I was in a room brimming with some suspicious people. There was a counter at which the receptionist was seated. I was a detective, relaxing with my fellow teammates in the anteroom. We were there to keep an eye on someone. Here someone was a lady, who was pretty and in her early forties. She was wearing a saree and was smartly dressed. She radiated vibes like the vamps in daily soaps but way smarter and more elegant. That place was a hotel that belonged to her. She was sitting on a sofa against us. She was waiting for someone. Suddenly a man came, tall and masculine.

They together went up to a room. I stalked the two to the second floor. To not be recognized, I disguised myself as a chef and slid into a pantry. They landed in an entrance hall connected with a pantry and staircases. That pantry had a service window through which I could see them. They were standing too close to each other. She positioned herself in a feminine way. I carefully tried to listen to their conversations.

"Darling, you know I don't like to wait, just give me that now." The man asserted.

I could not see them duly. Arduously I heard the woman saying, "I know James, here you go, but don't forget the contract!" She snickered. "This beautiful-blue substance will bring a catastrophe, and all the countries will bow in front of our boss." He asserted inhumanly. I had no idea what they were talking about, but I was sure their plans were wicked.

As I tried to scrutinize them, that woman saw me. Her eyes were full of suspicion. Conscience stricken, I jerked back and quickly planned an evacuation. I rushed in silence towards the balcony. With the help of a tent cloth, I descended and ran away with my team.

She had noticed me. She took a trip down memory lane and recalled my face. Vigilantly she summoned hooligans to chase and catch me to her. I somehow managed to be safe. A few weeks later, my cohort called and notified me about the ‘alert code’.

“They are going to hold a meeting in London, regarding a queer agreement!” He exclaimed in terror. Exigency was declared. We quickly packed our bags. Our agency provided us with the flight tickets.

Sooner we gathered in a famous shopping mall in London. Ironically, they were undertaking a secret mission in a public place. Our bunch of genius spies called ACID consisted of me (a 25-year-old woman), Bobby (a 24-year-old man), Milton (a 28-year-old man), and Dell (a 30-year-old man). These were our code names. Jamie was also one of our teammates; she was working as our undercover informer. She has tethered with us constantly.

We arrived at the Mall at different points and in different attires. I went into Clarks‘ showroom; it was big and labyrinth-like.

There, I joined Bobby. We acted as a married couple. Then a salesman interrupted and asked us, “would you like to try some sports shoes, sir? Your personality seems like a tough and sporty one! Or you might like some formals?”

Bobby hardly deigned to shake his head.

We were completely unaware of what next was about to happen to us. Spontaneously, my Bluetooth beeped a glitch sound and it got disconnected. Argus-eyed, I quickly glared at Bobby. He gave a similar reaction. Milton broke into us from nowhere and handed me a chit. It screamed, "They are approaching. Check and mate!" Those words sent chills up my spine. My heart was throbbing hard in my head, but as a trained person, I got a plan. Dell, outside the complex and in a car, was not identified yet. So, Bobby and I switched our genders, and Milton disguised themself as a salesman. Then we trudged out of the showroom, trying to behave normally. Bobby stole the clothes and wig of a mannequin. He was looking damn funny and unreal.

“You are looking jaw-dropping beautiful Bob!” Milton mocked him. Fortunately, my plan worked wonders. Somehow three of us managed to exit.

But the other side of the picture is still unexplained. Milton got caught. They took him along with them. They must have tortured him hard to get our information, or might even have beaten him up to death! Milton was a hero. He sacrificed his life for us. This incident was heartbreaking, unforgettable, and haunting for all of us.

Dell, Bobby, and I flew back to our country. Mysteriously, later that evening, Jamie informed me (on a telephonic call) that we had to withdraw our mission and no more investigations would take place regarding the virus agreement. It is uncanny that I never saw Jamie. I even heard about the 'virus' agreement for the first time! Maybe she was referring to that blue substance. But the question is how she knew about it. Even if she knew then why she didn't tell us about that. Her words cringed me for a while. My whole life seemed to be a lie to me. All these episodes propelled me to leave the agency. Therefore, I decided to live a life of solitude among the hills of Ooty.

The mystery is still unsolved!

CHAPTER TWO

Knocking Down Dead

It was a typical morning. Chiku and I were fighting over the remote of the television. Mumma was out of town, and dad went out to buy some food for us. Things didn't take even a little longer to turn upside down.

I suspected that some unusual commotion was coming from downstairs. I avoided at first but the commotion was followed by the screems of my dad. So, I rushed out to check. "Avni! save yourself, shut the door now!" dad wailed.

Blood was dripping off his hair. I was stunned. I had never been this much helpless ever before in my life. His screams sounded reverbed to me. His warnings were ineffective to me at that time. So he banged the door in my face to save me. The cruel creatures tore up his flesh with their sharp incisors.

"Nooo! dad, somebody please save him! Oh my god, dad!" I screamed hopelessly.

I realized that it was not the time to get overwhelmed by emotions. I ran inside the room quickly. I locked all the doors and switched off all the lights. These were similar creatures to those we see in the apocalypse movies. They seemed to be stronger than iron and steel. They were banging on the door dementedly. I was gasping.

My emergency senses got activated. I had to plan something as soon as possible. I took a bag pack and added some survival stuff to it; Water bottle, knife, ready-to-eat, belt, rubber band, whatever seemed important and crossed my way. I wrapped my arms with magazines and duct tape. My younger brother, who was just six years old, was frightened to death. I wrapped him in my arms and tried to jump out the window from the back of the house. The situation outside was even worse. It was a lose-lose situation. They could break in any minute. It was time to make a quick decision.

It could be a foolish step to go outside through the entrence. Hence, I vaulted out of the window, holding my brother in my arms.

People were running on the road insanely, intoxicated, coming towards me to eat me up like a beast. I fought with them, tired, gasping, energy-less, but managed to escape from them.

"Chiku, Are you okay?" an automated voice came out of my throat. He nodded innocently.

I quickly took a car abandoned on the roadside and started it.

"Bruh! I don't even know how to drive it!" My frustration-bound words showed my helplessness. I drove it uncontrollably. But in a twinkling, I took command of it. The car struck everything that came in its way.

Meanwhile, I realized that I drove too far. My heart was racing faster than I was driving the car. I tried to stop it, but due to my anxiety, I unconsciously stepped on the accelerator instead of the breaks. The car went out of my control.

“What the hell! How to stop this damn thing....come on Avni, you know, oh, no!” I sabotaged myself.

An idea hit my mind. I first tried to slow down the speed and then I pulled the hand breaks. I stepped out of the car, heaven-headed.

The place around me already seemed devastated and abandoned by humans and other living beings. Everything looked pale, lifeless, and destroyed. The ugly side of concrete jungles was protruding out.

Traumatized Chiku asked me, “are we safe now, di?” “Doesn’t seem so.” I sighed in grief.

CHAPTER THREE

A GRAVIDA WARRIOR

Warriors, spears, swords, and blood had encompassed me. Suddenly someone stabbed me on my back. I fell unconcious. A while later.

"uh! What's this...commotion? Wait. What am I doing in a battleground? Argh! that hurts! wait. Oh my God! I am pregnant. Where is... he?" I moaned.

"Hold back, ah! Hu...huff! I am coming out of the black. Did I.... fall unconscious?" I heaved.

"Rani Sahiba, are you okay?" the commander implored me.

" y..yeah! wait." I tried to get up. I felt dreadful cramps in my lower abdomen; I collapsed.

"Rani Sahiba!" He hurried towards me to grasp me. He poured a few drops of water into my maw and rubbed my palms.

"Rani Sahiba! Please get up. You have to win this battle, for the sake of this empire, for the sake of... majesty!" He was about to cry.

As soon as I heard the word majesty, I wide-opened my eyes. A wave of stimulation ran through my nerves. I supported my lower dantian with my hands. I rose. Like a true warrior, I mounted on the horse. With my sword in my right hand and the rein in my left hand and rode it dauntlessly.

My labor pains got severe and severe. I was sweating. My breath got intense. I killed the enemy soldiers one after another. However, progesterone kept driving me dejected and guilty for taking lives in front of my unborn child. Motherhood, patriotism, helplessness, dauntlessness, I suffered this jumble of emotions in consequence. My heart beat got faster and faster; my breath, heavier and heavier; my labor pain, deeper and deeper. But,

I couldn't stop. All I remembered was the promise that I made to the King.

He was a wise, rough, and able king. He was the best companion, I must say. He always had faith in me and my skills. He always encouraged me to take part in administration, and fencing. We used to spend quality time together honing our fencing skills. He always respected me, my choices, and my decisions. He went against the societal norms for me. I am forever grateful for having him in my life. Unfortunately, This beautiful dusk was followed by a hideous night. He got diagnosed with an incurable disease. His health deteriorated briskly. His organs started to malfunction. He could barely walk or stand straight. Since he was not able to look after the throne. He asked me to take over his responsibilities. He couldn't believe anyone else. I hesitated, but he found confidence in me. It was a tough time for both of us.

During our rough times, we saw a ray of hope and happiness. He was going to be a father. Joy once again found a place in our fort. We forgot all our worries and agony. The number of my valets was increased to take special care of me. God showered me with the strength to bear a child and maintain the vast kingdom at the same time.

However, in a twinkling, things turned upside down. Our enemies tried to take advantage of the situation. They started to build armies. They strategized to capture our Kingdom. We were informed by the diplomats to be alarmed and announced war. I wasn't psychically prepared. This news snatched away my sleep. I got intimidated.

One evening, when we were having our supper after a tiring day, the king held my hands firmly, he sighed, "Avni, I am sorry." he cracked in a heavy voice."I..." He tried to continue but something choked his throat. He looked down towards my feet. I chinned him up and signaled him to carry on. "I am feeling helpless, I am sorry, I can't be with you when you need me the most. I can't bear... this load, I don't know what to do now." He got impassioned. I felt a drop of tear on my feet.

"Your Majesty, please don't be broken. You are my strength. We walked through all the phases of life together, we shall get over this scenario too. I can't just watch you like this, direct me, what can I do for you?" I as well was broken inside but I tried to pursue him. He nodded and exhaled.

He looked into my eyes with hope and asked me, "will you give me a promise?" I nodded.

"Promise me, that you will never let this land fall into the hands of our enemies and show them that you are capable enough to be the administrator as well as a mother." I couldn't refuse his hope and confidence in me. I promised him that I would protect this kingdom no matter what.

"Aargh! oh no, it is the time!" Tears rolled on my cheeks, I roared through the pain and continued to kill the thousands of soldiers.

Now, the battle was over. The land we fought over was covered with corpses and blood. We won the battle. The commander and surviving soldiers rejoiced. I fainted. I was surrounded by darkness.

meanwhile.

"Please miss, save her. She is meant to be alive." The commander pleaded to my healer. I could hear the voices. My vision blurred. It was may be a camp. I was tired. My weakness was overpowering me.

I heared someone sobbing. They noticed that I came back to my senses. The doctor fed me some medicine and soup. She supported my back with a cushion. I could see the disappointed faces of the commander and soldiers in the room. My eyes searched for King.

"Rani Sahiba, We are extremely sorry to say this!" Sobbed the commander.

"What is this now?" I whispered in my cracked voice.

What he said next, just snatched away my soul from my body. He kneeled in front of me, turned his head down, and mumbled in a deep voice "Both, the infant prince and your majesty are no more!" He burst into tears and pleaded for apologies. I didn’t speak even a single word. My mind went blank. I had nothing to live for.

The next day, we left for the fort. Riding on our horses, While climbing on the fortress I noticed that the candles lightened up to celebrate our victory, flickered, and got extinguished automatically. I had only one thought lingering on my mind. "What's the use of such a win?"

CHAPTER FOUR

THE WICKED WITCH

An environment of trepidation encircled the village. The villagers lit up flambeau to save themselves from the darkness of death.

There, children were not allowed to leave their homes after 6 PM. They shut the windows and doors tight. The curtains were dropped and a haunted hush took over that village. It was none other than the repercussion of the fear of the wicked witch. She used to live in the woods on the outskirts of the countryside. She was petrified of the fire. Hence, the residents used to fence the village with flambeaus.

The villagers had to feed the witch one child a day. The younger the kid the more satisfied she felt. They had no other choice. She was very cunning. she never came out of the woods, but still had her fear maintained in the kernel of the residents of that village. She was an inordinate black magician.

One day, a man, tall and wise, maybe a vagabond, went there. That place was new to him. he introduced himself to the villagers as an explorer. He got to know about the wicked witch from the villagers. "Why don't you do something about it? Will you let your kids die this way? Even when you know her weakness!" He backlashed. Villagers were baffled by his response. They never thought that way. "This needs to be stopped otherwise one day will come when only oldies with no hopes will be left in this village!" these words worked as an eye-opener for them. Villagers found confidence in that man. They got eager and asked for a plan. He was self-assured that he would find a way. He asked for some time. Hours passed.

Now was the time to execute his plan. According to their schedule, they sent a child into the woods. As expected, that hag came out of her den to have some fleshy dinner. Despite being satisfied, she became furious. Guess why? that child was not a real one, it was a mannequin. The soil began to vibrate because of her anger. The villagers doubted their survival. They knew that her fury is going to destroy everything now. She got mad and ran to kill all of them. As soon as she stepped out of the jungle, her feet caught fire. That wise man had spilled the kerosene oil on the frontiers. He lit it up when she stepped on it. She got petrified of fire. She ran as fast as she could to save herself but within no time she was turned into ashes.

CHAPTER FIVE

THE OBLIVION OF LIFE

My aunt had thrown a house party. I was as always super excited. (My aunt is a pretty and friendly lady. Her daughter, Riya, is as tall as the Eiffel tower.) Her invitation reached me a week ago, and we had no interaction for days after receiving the invitation.

The-day arrived. I woke up early, took a shower, dressed casually, and packed my bag. We started our journey around 6 AM and reached her town at noon.

Her abode is not so usual. It's a Palace-like-Bungalow. It's coated in magnificent glimmery white. It has a swimming pool, a courtyard, a backyard, a front yard, Seven bedrooms, four washrooms, a kitchen, a dining hall, a guest room, a corridor, and a living room. A separate multipurpose hall also exists. Their house has decent-aesthetic decor.

This place was the first time haunting me. It was looking grim and denuded. No happiness, no cheer, and no life! I could sense the repelling force while gazing at it from outside. I advanced my steps to move inside.

A stretcher, painkillers, an oxygen cylinder, bandages, blood, and cuts were appallingly lying in the ghost-quiet room. My aunt was sprawling there wounded egregiously. The doctor was trying to gather her to life. She was struggling for a single breath, for a single heartbeat. My Uncle ran towards my dad and wrapped him up in his arms. He started whining. This was a shock for me. Tears rolled down my cheeks. Nothing could save her, not even the money and comfort they enjoyed all their life. This scene made me meet the reality of this world. Thinking that the sight might thwack me, my parents asked me to go inside Riya's bedroom.

She was resting inexpressively. The noise of my steps brought her out of her oblivion. Throughout the day, we had no chatter and movement.

When it started to grow dark, a voice summoned us, "Avni, Riya, step down for dinner!" As I was craning down, I noticed that everything that I saw earlier was not there anymore! As if nothing happened. My mind was blown out. I went back upstairs to Riya, she was not there. I ran back down to my mum, and she was not the one I had known! I tried to escape that bungalow but couldn't. Suddenly the electricity went off, and I fell unconscious in the darkness.

CHAPTER SIX

SERPENT GODDESS

I was looking out the window of a cottage built on a mountain cliff, covered with grey clouds, grey skeleton-like trees, and a grey-blue sky. The scenery was depressing. It was all cloudy and I could hear thunderous sounds continuously. To a pluviophile like me, this environment wasn't pleasant at all.

The ghostly silence broke when, a fragile voice came afar, maybe from the kitchen. "Sayyeshaa, get ready asap, we have to start the prep for the procession of the serpent goddess!"

"Sayyesha? This name is new to me. Serpent goddess? I don't know who she is." These thoughts were lingering in my mind.

Suddenly my cousin's sister, who is a part of this tribe exclaimed, "don't think so loud Sayyesha!" I was stunned. How could she know what I was thinking?

She continued, "Don't worry it's common here. It's because you have been living in the city far from here since birth, this place and this name are new to you, but it is your real name. Sayyesha." "This outlined community is unexplored by you but don't worry, I am with you." Her words comforted me.

As soon as I eased off, she exclaimed, "Sayyu, be cautious. It is the most dangerous ritual of our tribe!"

She added, "People say that some iniquitous forces might hinder the process and, ifff...even a single, minute, trivial inaccuracy is committed by anyone during it, the result could be catastrophic for *yajmana*." Her expressions grew pale.

"But why me? Why am I the host?" I was getting cowardly curious.

She replied, "because this ritual, procession to the temple of serpent goddess is performed only for those who either have her clemency and exceptional blessings or are under her evil eyes. Who knows what's your case." After completing her words she left the room.

I could feel my palpitations. A slender-straight frequency passed through my ears. This blandness of mine was interrupted by the tumult of sticks hitting the drums and tribals shouting in front of my house.

My mother helped me in getting ready for the cavalcade. After reciting a few prayers we started our journey. The journey was about two weeks long. We stayed at our relatives‘ and acquaintances' abodes during the nights and proceeded towards the temple during the morning. Subsequently, we covered a distance of 3,218 meters, and in the fullness of time, we reached our destination. I counted on my safety. I believed that the serpent goddess had mercy on me because snakes and serpents seemed to be friends with me. It was only me who spotted them anywhere (my friends used to think that I might have lost my head) but they (snakes) didn't ever hurt me. That couldn't be a mere coincidence.

Thankfully, all the steps and sequences for my exorcism were completed successfully. Afterward, we offered some fruits, delicacies, milk, ornaments, flowers, and clothes to her idol. I noticed a few poor kids hiding their malnutritioned naked bodies behind the pillars of the temple. The place was abandoned by us once the final prayers were offered to her. I got to know by hearing from two ladies of the village that the objects offered to her get disappeared without leaving a trace behind. I interpreted this as a good way of donating to the poor or needy without disturbing their pride.

A Note To Readers

Dear reader,

Each of these stories you've just read has a back story. If you, as a reader, are interested to know more about what must have happened next or what might have been the reason behind a particular sequence, then you may let me know your opinion here:

avnifiranker@gmail.com

Printed by Libri Plureos GmbH in Hamburg, Germany

9 798888 151013